To my dad
—A.B.

For John and Mandi
with much love
—V.F.

Text copyright © 1995 by Vivian French
Illustrations copyright © 1995 by Alison Bartlett
First American Edition 1995 published by Orchard Books
First published in Great Britain in 1995 by Hodder Children's Books

Orchard Books
95 Madison Avenue
New York, NY 10016

Manufactured in Singapore
Book design by Jean Krulis

10 9 8 7 6 5 4 3 2 1

The text of this book is set in Bembo.
The illustrations are acrylic paintings.

Library of Congress Cataloging-in-Publication Data
French, Vivian.
Oliver's vegetables / Vivian French ; illustrated by Alison
Bartlett. — 1st American ed.
p.   cm.
Summary: While visiting his grandfather, who has a wonderful
garden, Oliver learns to eat vegetables other than potatoes.
ISBN 0-531-09462-6
[1. Food habits—Fiction.   2. Vegetables—Fiction.
3. Grandfathers—Fiction.]   I. Bartlett, Alison, ill.   II. Title.
PZ7.F8891701   1995   [E]—dc20   94-45475

Oliver's Vegetables

by Vivian French · illustrated by Alison Bartlett

Orchard Books • New York

"Finish up, Oliver," said his mother,
"or we'll miss the bus."
"Can't we walk to Grandpa's house?"
asked Oliver.
"No," said his mother. "It's too far.
Hurry up!"

The best thing about Grandpa's house was the wonderful garden.
"I grow all my own vegetables," Grandpa said proudly.

"I don't eat vegetables," Oliver told Grandpa.
"I only eat french fries."
"If you want french fries," said Grandpa, "you must find
the potatoes. If you find something else, you eat that
and no complaints. Is it a bargain?"

Oliver ran around the garden, but he couldn't see any potatoes. "They must be hiding," he said, and pulled at the nearest leaves. "Carrots," said Grandpa. "Just the thing for Monday supper." That night Oliver ate his first carrots.

Oliver took a long time making up his
mind on Tuesday. Gran and Grandpa
came to watch him.
"Those crinkly leaves are pretty,"
he said at last. "Are the potatoes there?"
"Spinach," said Grandpa.
They had spinach for supper.
"That *was* good,"
said Oliver.

On Wednesday Oliver got up early.
"Potatoes are very important," he said, "so they
must have big leaves." HERE THEY ARE!"
Grandpa smiled. "That's rhubarb."
They had rhubarb pie that evening.
"That was very good," said Oliver.

It rained on Thursday. When it
stopped, Oliver hurried outside.
"Have you found the potatoes?"
Grandpa asked.
"No," said Oliver. "I've found
slugs and snails.
Are they eating my potatoes?"
Grandpa shook his head.
"That's cabbage."
Oliver had two helpings.
"Very, very good,"
he said.

On Friday Oliver was sure that he had found the potatoes. When he pulled at the leaves, up came a bunch of beets. Oliver ate all of his beet salad. "Very, very, very good," he said.

On Saturday Oliver
played soccer.
The ball landed
in a tangle
of sticks and leaves.
Oliver was sure the
potatoes weren't there,
and Grandpa nodded.
"Peas," he said.
Oliver had three helpings
of pea soup that evening.
"Was it good?"
asked Grandpa.
"No," said Oliver,
"it was delicious!"

Oliver rushed into the garden on Sunday.
"HERE THEY ARE!"
"How did you know?" asked Grandpa.
"They were the only things left," said Oliver.

"Can we have french fries now?" Oliver asked.
"You scrub the potatoes," said Gran,
"and I'll peel them. Grandpa
can cut them up."

Oliver, Gran, and Grandpa sat down to eat.
The door opened and in walked Oliver's mother.
She saw the plate of french fries.
"Oh dear. I did hope Oliver would eat something
different while he was here," she said.
Oliver and Grandpa looked at each other.
His mother stared as they laughed
and laughed and laughed.